The NOSE BOOK

BY AL PERKINS

ILLUSTRATED BY

Roy McKie

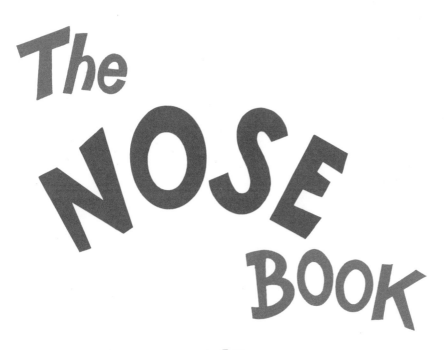

A Bright & Early Book

RANDOM HOUSE / NEW YORK

This title was originally catalogued by the Library of Congress as follows:
Perkins, Al. The nose book. Illustrated by Roy McKie.
New York, Random House [1970] 28 p. col. illus. 24 cm.
(A Bright and early book, BE8)
Noses are interesting and serve many purposes including the one of holding up glasses.
[1. Stories in rhyme] I. McKie, Roy, illus. II. Title.
PZ8.3.P42No [E] 71-117540 ISBN 0-394-80623-9 ISBN 0-394-90623-3 (lib. bdg.)

Manufactured in the United States of America 45 44 43 42 41 40 39 38 37

Everybody
grows
a nose.

I see a nose
on every face.

I see noses
every place!

A nose
between
each pair of eyes.

Noses!
Noses!
Every size.

They grow
on every
kind of head.

They come in blue . . .

. . . and pink

. . . and red.

Some are
very, very long.

Some are
very, very strong.

Everywhere a fellow goes,
he sees some
new, new kind of nose.

A nose is useful.
After all . . .

some play horns . . .

. . . and some play ball.

A nose is good
for making holes

. . . in trees

. . . and roofs

. . . and barber poles.

But sometimes
noses aren't much fun.
They sniffle.

They get burned by sun.

A nose gets punched . . .

. . . and bumped on doors

. . . and bumped on walls

. . . and bumped on floors!

Sometimes
your nose
will make you sad.
Sometimes
your nose
will make you mad.

BUT . . .

Just suppose
you had no nose!

Then you
could never
smell
a rose . . .

. . . or pie, or chicken a la king.

You'd never smell a single thing.

And one thing more.
Suppose . . . no nose . . .

Where would
all our glasses sit?
They'd all fall off!
Just THINK of it!

And that's why
everybody grows,
between his eyes,
some kind of nose!